S0-ABN-017

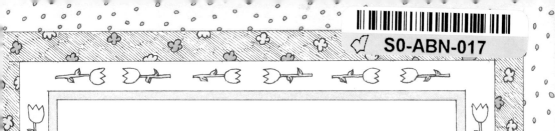

Millicent Maybe

by Ellen Weiss

AN EASY-READ STORY BOOK

Franklin Watts
New York | London | 1979

R.L. 2.1 Spache Revised Formula

Library of Congress Cataloging in Publication Data

Weiss, Ellen.
  Millicent Maybe.

  (An Easy-read story book)
  SUMMARY: Indecisive Millicent, who has
trouble making up her mind, discovers what she
thinks is a permanent solution — only to experience
real chaos.
  [1. Decision making — Fiction] I. Title.
PZ7.W4472Mi   [E]   78-13144
ISBN 0-531-02382-6
ISBN 0-531-02299-4 lib. bdg.

Copyright © 1979 by Ellen Weiss
All rights reserved
Printed in the United States of America
6   5   4   3   2

Millicent Maybe

Millicent Maybe lived all by herself.

She could cook what she pleased.

And buy what she pleased.

And go where she pleased.

But she could never
make up her mind.

"What should I eat?"

said Millicent each morning.

"Maybe cornflakes.

Or maybe pancakes.

Or maybe toast and jam."

Millicent could not decide.

So she ate a little of this
and a little of that.

"What should I wear today?"
said Millicent.
"Maybe it will rain.
  Or maybe it will be sunny.
  Maybe it will be cold.
  Or maybe it will be hot."
Millicent could not decide.

So she wore a little of this
and a little of that.

It was maybe this or maybe that
at the library,

and at the sweet shop,

and at the shoe store.

And the supermarket drove her crazy!

Soon Millicent had eaten too much
of this and too much of that.
She could not fit into her clothes.

She had bought too much of this
and too much of that.
There was hardly enough room
left for Millicent!

"If only I had someone
to tell me what to do!"
cried Millicent.

Just then she saw an ad
in the newspaper:

"Hooray!" shouted Millicent.
"That's just what I need!"
And she ran to the pet shop.

But there were so many parrots.
Millicent could not decide
which one to buy.

So she took them all.

"I'll never have to make up
my mind again," said Millicent.

"These parrots will tell me
what to do!"

And they did.

As soon as she got home

the yellow parrot

began to shout,

"TAKE A BATH! TAKE A BATH!"

"Whatever you say!"

said Millicent.

And she ran upstairs

to fill the tub.

Then the green
parrot shouted,

"MAKE POPCORN!! POPCORN!"

"Whatever you say!"
said Millicent.
And she ran downstairs
to the kitchen.

"STAND ON YOUR HEAD!"

squawked the blue parrot.
"Whatever you say!"
said Millicent.

And she turned upside down.

Suddenly she heard
Splash! Splash! Splash!
Pop! Pop! Pop!

"Oh, no!" said Millicent.
"My bath! My popcorn!
I forgot all about them!"

"Help!" shouted Millicent.

"What should I do?"

"GO TO SLEEP!"

"Quiet!" shouted Millicent.

"I never heard anything so silly!"

Then, for the first time in her life,
Millicent made up her mind.
She opened the window.
"Bye-bye, parrots!" said Millicent.
"I can think for myself!"

She opened the front door.

All the furniture

and all the clothes

and all the food

floated out of the house.

Then Millicent floated out, too.

Everyone came running to help.
"Shall we carry it all back inside?"
they asked.
"No, thank you," said Millicent.
"I don't need a little of this
and a little of that.
I'll choose what I like best."

Millicent decided what to keep
and what to give away.

The more she decided,
the easier it got.

Then Millicent sat down
in her softest chair.
She wore her prettiest dress
and her very best hat.
She thought of all the things
she used to have.
And she didn't miss them a bit!